STEAMPUNK CITY

An Alphabetical Journey

· VISITOR ·

NAME: _____

DATE: _____

POW!

BROOKLYN

Published by POW! a division of powerHouse Cultural Entertainment, Inc.
37 Main Street, Brooklyn, NY 11201-1021

info@POWkidsbooks.com

www.POWkidsbooks.com
www.powerHousePackaging.com
www.powerHouseBooks.com

Library of Congress Control Number: 2014937066

ISBN 978-1-57687-703-6

10 9 8 7 6 5 4 3 2 1

Printed in China

STEAMPUNK CITY

An Alphabetical Journey

Manuel Šumberac

Text by Benjamin Mott

A

IS FOR AERODROME,
WHERE AIRSHIPS GO TO DOCK

IS FOR THE BONEYARDS,
WHERE CONSTRUCTION NEVER STOPS

is for the Cyclotron,
which makes all our power

IS FOR DEFENDER,
THE HIGHEST OF TOWERS

is the Edging Works,
Keeping roads paved

IS FOR FABRICATOR,
WHERE MACHINES ARE ALL MADE

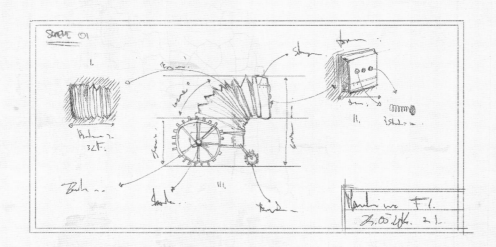

G

IS THE GRAVITY DECK,
KEEPING FEET ON THE GROUND

IS FOR HALL OF HEALTH,
TO MAKE US ALL SOUND

I IS THE IRRIGATOR,
WHICH KEEPS THE CROPS WATERED

IS FOR JUNK BARGE,
WHERE SALVAGE IS BARTERED

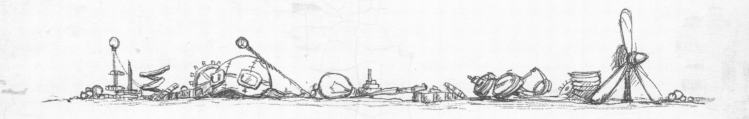

is the Kaleidoscope,
where dreams come to life

IS FOR LINKAGE,
WHERE ALL WASTE IS PIPED

IS THE METROCORE,
AT THE CENTER OF THE CITY

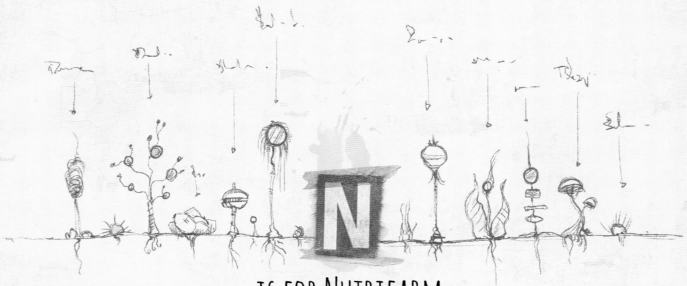

IS FOR NUTRIFARM,
WHERE FOOD GROWS APLENTY

IS THE OMNIFIELD,
WHERE MOST EVERYTHING'S LEARNED

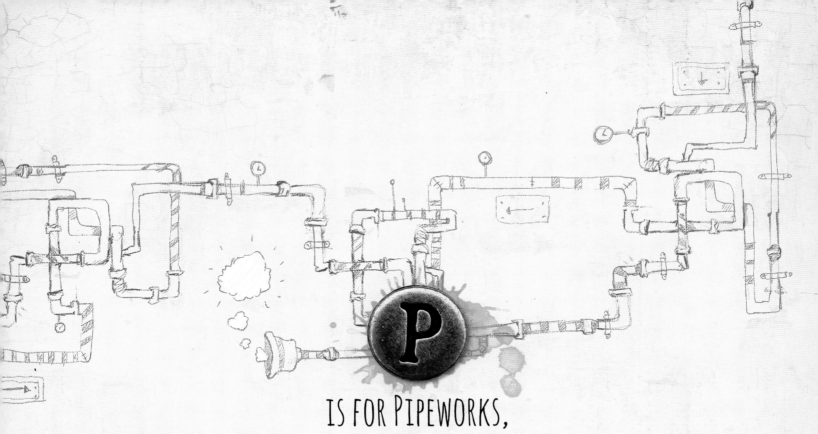

IS FOR Pipeworks,
THROUGH WHICH THOUGHTS ARE TRANSFERRED

Q is the Questorium,
where journeys begin

IS FOR THE REUNITER,
FINDING LOST KIN

IS THE STEAM TANK,

WHICH KEEPS LIQUIDS BOILED

T

is for Tesla Transfer,

where electrons are coiled

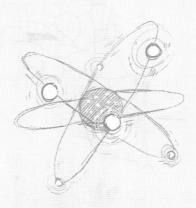

IS THE UNDERTANK,
FOR STORING GROUNDWATER

IS FOR VITAMIX,
WHICH MAKES US MUCH SMARTER

is for Wind Watchers,
who name every breeze

X

IS THE Xebec,
FOR CROSSING THE SEAS

Y

is for Yeasayer,
who opened our eyes

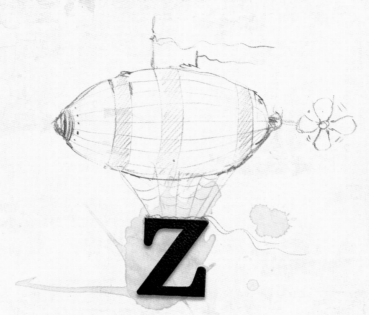

z

IS THE ZEPPELIN,
WHICH CONQUERED THE SKIES

ArTiSt's NoTe

I am grateful to the following people for their assistance, support and patience during this project: my parents Josip i Palmira Šumberac, my brothers Danijel and Kristijan, my girlfriend Andrea Sužnjević. Special thanks to Kirsten Hall and the whole team at Bright Agency for their help in making this book come to life. Huge thanks to POW! for all their efforts in publishing and promoting this book. And of course big thanks to everyone who supported this idea, who encouraged me and who had faith from my first drawing to the final product. Thank you!

Bio

Manuel Šumberac is a native of Pula, Croatia, where he was born in 1988. He graduated from the Academy of Fine Arts in Zagreb, where he studied in the Department of Animation and New Media. Manuel has worked extensively in film, including as lead animator on Zdenko Bašić's short film *Guliver* (2009) and Livio Rajh's *Industry* (2013). Manuel has created his own animated shorts: *Escargot* (2010), *In the Shadow*, *The Oars* (both 2011), and *Clockwork Heart* (2013). Manuel's illustrations have appeared in several picture books, including *Pinocchio*, *Snow White*, *The Snow Queen*, *The Night Before Christmas*, *A Midsummer Night's Dream*, *Steampunk Poe*, and *Steampunk Frankenstein*. Manuel lives in Zagreb, Croatia. Read more about him at www.manuelsumberac.com.

Benjamin Mott is a children's book writer and editor who lives in Brooklyn, New York.